SHADOW
SQUADRON

BLACK ANCHOR

STONE ARCH BOOKS
a capstone imprint

2013.671

SHADOW
SQUADRON

BLACK ANCHOR

WRITTEN BY
CARL BOWEN

ILLUSTRATED BY
WILSON TORTOSA

COLORED BY
BENNY FUENTES

2012.241

Shadow Squadron is published by
Stone Arch Books,
A Capstone Imprint,
1710 Roe Crest Drive
North Mankato, MN 56003
www.capstonepub.com

Cataloging-in-Publication Data is available
on the Library of Congress website.

ISBN: 978-1-4342-4605-9 (library binding)
ISBN: 978-1-4342-6111-3 (eBook)

Summary: A Chinese oil rig platform near
Cuban waters has been hijacked, forcing
Shadow Squadron to intervene. But before
Lieutenant Commander Cross and his men
can board the *Black Anchor*, they learn the
hijackers are American mercenaries, and
they've taken hostages.

Designed by Brann Garvey

2019.681

Printed in the United States of America
in Brainerd, Minnesota.
092012   006938BANGS13

CONTENTS

2012.101

ACCESS GRANTED

SHADOW SQUADRON DOSSIER

CROSS, RYAN

RANK: Lieutenant Commander
BRANCH: Navy SEAL
PSYCH PROFILE: Cross is the team leader of Shadow Squadron. Control oriented and loyal, Cross insisted on hand-picking each member of his squad.

WALKER, ALONSO

RANK: Chief Petty Officer
BRANCH: Navy SEAL
PSYCH PROFILE: Walker is Shadow Squadron's second-in-command. His combat experience, skepticism, and distrustful nature make him a good counter-balance to Cross's leadership.

YAMASHITA, KIMIYO

RANK: Lieutenant
BRANCH: Army Ranger
PSYCH PROFILE: The team's sniper is an expert marksman and a true stoic. It seems his emotions are as steady as his trigger finger.

BRIGHTON, EDGAR

RANK: Staff Sergeant
BRANCH: Air Force Combat Controller
PSYCH PROFILE: The team's technician and close-quarters-combat specialist is popular with his squadmates but often agitates his commanding officers.

PHOTO NOT AVAILABLE

4236.052

LARSSEN, NEIL

RANK: Second Lieutenant
BRANCH: Army Ranger
PSYCH PROFILE: Neil prides himself on being a jack-of-all-trades. His versatility allows him to fill several roles for Shadow Squadron.

PHOTO NOT AVAILABLE

1216.052

SHEPHERD, MARK

RANK: Lieutenant
BRANCH: Army (Green Beret)
PSYCH PROFILE: The heavy-weapons expert of the group, Shepherd's love of combat borders on unhealthy.

2019.681

CLASSIFIED

MISSION BRIEFING

OPERATION

BLACK ANCHOR 1234

We've just received a report that a Chinese oil rig platform in Cuban waters has been hijacked. Strangely, the hijackers are American mercenaries, and they've taken the workers hostage. To make matters worse, the Cuban military is on its way, and they have no concern for the lives of anyone on board. We can fully expect the Chinese military to intervene in short order, as well. If that happens, we'll have an international incident on our hands, and that's simply not an option. That means we need to get in, get the hostages, neutralize the mercs, and get out. Fast.

— Lieutenant Commander Ryan Cross

3245.98

GULF OF MEXICO

PRIMARY OBJECTIVE(S)

- Secure the oil rig platform and transport hostages to safety

1932.789

SECONDARY OBJECTIVE(S)

- Minimize damage done to Hardwall mercenaries

- Avoid contact with the Cuban and Chinese forces

0412.981

1624.054

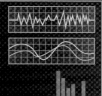

INTEL

DECRYPTING
IIIIIIIII   IIIIIIIIIIIIIII

12345

COM CHATTER

- BLACK OP – a black op, or operation, is a covert, secret mission

- REBREATHER – apparatus used to breathe under water

- NAVY SEAL – member of the Sea, Air, and Land teams that function as the US government's primary special operations force

- SDV – swimmer delivery vehicle, or a manned underwater submersible

3245.98 ● ● ●

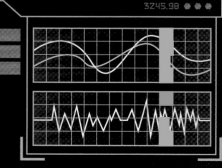

CHAPTER ONE

BLACK ANCHOR

The black salt water engulfed Chief Petty Officer Alonso Walker on all sides. He was in his element — both literally and figuratively. As a child, Walker had believed that the black depths of the ocean were filled with giant monsters like the Kraken, the Leviathan, and Moby Dick.

But now, as an adult, Walker knew there were few creatures in the sea more dangerous than himself. After all, he had been an elite career soldier of the US Navy. Now he was second-in-command of Shadow Squadron, and beside him floated a real, modern-day sea monster, the USS *Georgia*. It ws a 600-foot-long, Ohio-class nuclear submarine.

His present state had been a long time in the making. After coasting through twelve years of school with near perfect grades, Walker shocked his friends and family by enlisting in the Navy the day after graduation.

From the beginning, Walker had his sights set on joining the legendary SEALs. After a grueling trip through the SEAL training program, he'd earned himself a place on Team Two based out of Little Creek, Virginia. He served with distinction through multiple tours, climbing up the ranks and piling up the medals. And making the world a better, safer place in the best way he knew how.

His skillful and honorable service caught the US Special Operations Command's attention. Officers there selected Walker for inclusion in its top-level, top secret, experimental missions unit: Shadow Squadron.

As part of the elite unit of trainees, Walker worked with special operations personnel from every branch of the military. For several years now, he'd traveled throughout he world to perform top secret black ops against nothing less than the forces of evil. He was probably too old to think of his job in such corny terms, but in his heart he still believed in the righteousness of the work he did. And he believed that if his friends and family back home knew about the work he did, they'd be proud of him.

If they saw him here and now, floating in these frigid, black waters, Walker wondered if his loved ones would be worried about him.

Walker was in the early stages of a mission, floating alongside the mighty leviathan *USS Georgia*. The vessel loomed in the water like one of the imaginary monsters of Walker's childhood. But here in the otherwise empty darkness, Walker found the sub's presence to be comforting, not frightening.

Sucking recycled air through his rebreather, Walker kick-stroked to the rear of the bullet-shaped Dry Deck Shelter near the *Georgia*. The DDS's circular rear hatch stood open. At the moment, four of his teammates were carefully sliding a black, torpedo-shaped vessel out into the ocean.

The vessel was a Swimmer Delivery Vehicle, though SEALs like Walker preferred to think of them as SEAL Delivery Vehicles. It served as an open submersible that could carry up to eight soldiers undetected. The SDV could travel distances greater than any person could reasonably be expected to swim, especially in frigid ocean waters. Walker had trained on SDVs for as long as he'd been a SEAL, and he and his fellow SDV soldiers secretly considered themselves to be a cut above even their "vanilla" SEAL brethren.

While Walker was no slouch at land navigation or airborne insertion, he was most at home in the water. He'd worked hard to see that every man on Shadow Squadron — especially those who'd come from the Army, Marines, and Air Force — completed their combat swimmer training with only the highest marks. He was still undoubtedly the best and most experienced combat swimmer on the unit, but he had total faith in his men's capabilities beneath the waves.

Of course, they weren't really his men, he had to admit. The JSOC had seen fit to recruit and saddle him with a new commanding officer: Lieutenant Commander Daniel Cross.

It rankled Walker. Cross hadn't been in the Navy as long as he had. Cross hadn't been a SEAL as long as he had. Cross had combat experience, but not as much as Walker had. And worst of all, Cross wasn't even an SDV SEAL — he was pure "vanilla" SEAL. Before being recruited into Shadow Squadron, Cross had done more mountaineering and arctic survival training than SDV training.

So why did the JSOC put this man in charge of Shadow Squadron? Walker wondered.

On the positive side, Cross ran a clean op. Shadow Squadron hadn't lost a single man — so far. They'd faced pirates off the Somali coast, accomplishing their mission with slick professionalism and impressive flexibility. Walker worried, though, that their early successes were going to Cross's head.

Cross had come to Shadow Squadron with a reputation as a hero and a natural leader. In Walker's experience, that almost always went hand in hand with stubbornness and over-confidence. So far, the lieutenant commander listened to input, and he suffered disagreement pretty well, but he was quick to halt discussion when he felt his point had been proven. True, Walker probably could argue with his CO a little less, but the man just seemed *too* smug. It was hard not to want to put him in his place once in a while.

But Commander Cross was right more often than he was wrong. That only made him all the more annoying.

Thankfully, Walker's sense of professionalism ensured that he put his feelings aside when the team was in the field. The men needed to see unity in their ranks. If he, the second-in-command, was always second-guessing and arguing with Cross, it would unsettle the others. A lack of focus would likely end up getting someone killed. So no matter what he thought of Cross personally, Walker knew he wouldn't be able to continue his service with another man's death on his conscience.

That didn't mean Walker had to keep his opinions to himself before Shadow Squadron's missions got underway, though . . .

* * *

Earlier that day, at dawn, Cross gathered his eight-man Shadow Squadron unit in the base ready room. The smell of fresh coffee hang thick in the air as all the other well-groomed men wearing camouflage fatigues shook off the morning weariness.

Cross, on the other hand, seemed to have plenty of energy. It was just one more reason for Walker to dislike him: Cross was a morning person.

"We've got a situation," Cross said energetically. He tapped on the computer-operated whiteboard on the wall and synced up with the room's tablet computer. "This one hits pretty close to home."

That got the men's attention. Ever since the events of 9/11, the fear of further terrorist action on American soil had loomed large over the nation. None were more sensitive to the terrorist threat than those in the military.

"I'm sure you're all familiar with the problems brewing in the waters just off Cuba," Cross said. He brought up a satellite map of the Gulf of Mexico, focusing on its eastern half.

Walker knew what Cross was referring to, but a quick glance at the other six men showed him that not everyone else understood.

The team's youngest member, the Air Force Combat Controller Staff Sergeant Edgar Brighton, raised his hand. "Sorry, Commander," he said, not looking sorry at all. "I get all my news from Jon Stewart and Stephen Colbert."

A few chuckles came from the other men. Walker glared at the young man, shaming Brighton and silencing the others. Brighton was a brave soldier and a technical genius, but he seemed to see himself as a class clown. Walker thought that was unbecoming conduct for an elite soldier.

"Sorry, Chief Walker," Brighton mumbled, having the decency to at least look embarrassed. He turned back to face Cross. "All the same, I'm still not quite sure what you're referring to, sir."

"It's all right," Cross said, taking it far too easy on Brighton for Walker's tastes. If Cross didn't make an example out of Brighton, the other men would start thinking it was okay to be so casual. Cross tapped and swiped for a second on the tablet computer, bringing up an overlay on the whiteboard. Green and yellow zones showed up surrounding the coasts of the United States and Cuba. A blue zone appeared over the coast of Mexico. A roughly triangular gap appeared in the Gulf where the three zones didn't quite reach one another.

"For a few years now," Cross said, "the Chinese government has been negotiating with what's left of the Castro regime in Cuba for rights to drill for oil and natural gas in Cuba's territorial waters. Last month, Cuba agreed, and China set up its *Hēi Máo* gas and oil platform in the eastern Gulf of Mexico."

"*Hēi Máo* means *Black Anchor* in the Chinese language," Walker added.

Cross nodded, then tapped his tablet again. A red dot appeared in the northwestern part of the yellow zone with the words *Black Anchor* above it. Cross pointed at the red dot which was right next to the triangular gap. "It's Cuba's right to choose who they share their resources with, but their zone is right next to ours," he said. "For some folks in Congress, having

the Chinese float a GOPLAT in the Gulf at all makes them . . . uneasy."

That's an understatement, Walker thought. There was an awful lot of oil and natural gas buried beneath the Gulf of Mexico, but not every source was partitioned neatly. Quite often, more than one country had access to a reserve, causing tension between nations. Even worse, sometimes oil sources overlapped boundaries. That was a negotiations nightmare for all the countries involved.

"I can't say I'm thrilled about the situation either, Commander," Brighton said.

"Normally, this sort of thing is handled by the suits in Washington," Cross said, "But then yesterday, something happened." With another swipe across his tablet, the red dot on the whiteboard drifted northward. When the red dot crossed into the triangular region on the map, it vanished. "Yesterday the *Black Anchor* drifted into this doughnut hole here, then went dark."

A glance around gave Walker the impression that Cross's supposedly dramatic comment had just left the men even more confused. Walker stood up, taking it upon himself to clarify the situation.

"The 'doughnut hole' is the spot between where the exclusive economic zones offshore of the United Stats, Mexico, and Cuba don't quite meet up together," Walker explained. "Arguing over ownership of the doughnut hole has been relatively quiet until China and Cuba started fighting over it recently."

"So how did this GOPLAT get installed there?" Brighton asked.

"It's not a fixed platform," Walker answered before Cross could. "It's a floating oil rig. It's supposed to be held in place by a set of anchors, but if the anchors are up, it can move around freely. That's part of the reason Congress put so much pressure on the President to raise a fuss when the Chinese put the *Black Anchor* where they did. They figured it was just a matter of time before the platform 'accidentally' ended up in the doughnut hole. Looks like Congress was right."

"Sounds like the President has a doughnut hole in his head," Brighton joked.

"That's your government you're talking about," Walker said sharply. "Show some respect."

"Sorry, Chief," Brighton said. He looked at Cross, as if seeking support. To his credit, Cross looked rather peeved at the young man, as well. Noting this, Brighton sat up straight. He added, "So when you say this thing went dark, Commander, I'm guessing it didn't really disappear."

"Nope," Cross said, changing the whiteboard display once more. It now showed an ocean-level view of the Chinese GOPLAT, as seen from several miles away. A set of map coordinates and a time stamp from the previous day appeared in the corner of the screen. The platform looked like an array of metal scaffoldings with a huge crane on top.

"We know exactly where it is — that isn't the problem," Cross said. "The *Black Anchor* radioed for resupply early last week, but since the resupply vessel came and went, all communication ceased."

"Do we know what happened?" Walker asked. He was still standing at the front of the ready room next to Cross even though he had nothing further to add.

"We didn't know until last night," Cross replied. "Shortly after the resupply vessel left, an unmarked speedboat showed up. It moored to the rig without permission and a team of armed men climbed aboard. They stormed the rig and took the crew hostage."

"Pirates again?" Brighton said. "I didn't even know the Gulf had pirates."

"They're not pirates," Cross said, his tone growing grim. "They're American mercenaries."

That statement blew away the last of the morning haze in the men. Their eyes grew wide and alert now.

Cross tapped his computer tablet once more, bringing up a file photo of a square-jawed blond man in his thirties. Below the picture was a corporate logo for some company called Hardwall Security.

"This is Corbin Van Sant," Cross said. "He and the attackers are private security contractors employed by Hardwall Security. The company's website claims they specialize in providing security at sea all around the world. Their 'onboard security experts' get paid to ride along with merchant vessels or escort ships to protect clients from pirates and other criminals. They also occasionally patrol the coastlines at home for what they call 'unwelcome visitors.'"

"Like the vigilantes along the US-Mexico border," said Mark Shepherd.

"Except these guys are highly trained and efficient," Cross said.

"In other words, dangerous," said Walker.

Cross nodded. "They made headlines a few years ago for exposing a South American drug smuggling operation," he said. "But they spend most of their time searching for boats transporting illegal immigrants. The company's founder, Corbin Van Sant, has a reputation for a tough anti-immigration stance. He seems to think it's his personal mission to 'protect the sanctity of America's borders and waters.'"

"Sounds like a racist," one of the men mumbled. Walker saw it was Second Lieutenant Neil Larssen, one of the squadron's Rangers.

"So what happened, exactly?" Walker asked, redirecting the conversation. The more interruptions Cross allowed, the further off track this briefing would get. "This Corbin Van Sant character just suddenly decided to go from American patriot to international pirate?"

"Specifics are sketchy," Cross said. "What we know so far is that Van Sant had one of his boats watching the *Black Anchor*. He sent it over the second the platform left Cuba's waters. His men probably tried to intimidate the Chinese into going back the way they came, and when the Chinese refused, things got out of hand. Now we have a hostage situation. We don't know any other details, though. For all I know, Van Sant's guys came to the platform with every intention of hijacking it."

"How do we know this much in the first place, sir?" asked Lieutenant Kimiyo Yamashita, the team's sniper. The stoic Army Ranger rarely spoke during mission briefings, which Walker appreciated, but something about this mission had apparently piqued his curiosity. "Have the Cubans asked us for help resolving it? Or the Chinese?"

"No," Cross admitted. "The Chinese argue that the doughnut hole in the Gulf is in international waters. They believe they're within their rights. We only learned what we know from —"

"Spying?" Yamashita interrupted. He said it in a flat tone, without judgment.

"Yep," Cross confirmed matter-of-factly. "Now, obviously, American citizens taking Chinese and Cuban nationals hostage is a big problem. Everybody's trying to keep it out of the news for now, but there's only so long that's going to be in the victims' best interests. When the press gets wind of this, the United States is going to end up looking bad. The Chinese and Cubans are trying to negotiate with Van Sant's people, but we believe they're just stalling until they can mount a rescue operation. When they do, we'll be facing a major international incident."

"Not that we aren't already," Walker put in.

"Which is where we come in," Cross said. "We're going to board the *Black Anchor* before anyone else can, free those prisoners, and deal with the Hardwall mercs who took them hostage."

"Deal with them?" Brighton asked. "You mean like . . ." He pointed his finger to his temple.

"I'm hoping it doesn't come to that," Cross said.

"With all due respect," Walker said, "these are American citizens we're talking about."

"They are criminals," Cross said.

"American criminals, sir," Walker added. "We should take every effort to capture them alive so they can stand trial."

"These men are terrorizing foreign nationals in the name of one man's political agenda," Cross said. "They're an embarrassment to what our country stands for. If they force our hand, I will not make it easy for them."

"All the same —" Walker began.

"This isn't a discussion, Chief," Cross said sternly. "Now sit down. We have some work to do."

* * *

Walker's pride still stung as they traveled in the SDV. He wasn't normally the type to sulk, and was disappointed in himself for not just shrugging it off and carrying on as normal.

But now wasn't the time to feel sorry for himself. From here on out, floating in the moonlit waters, the team was on noise discipline until the hostages and mercenaries were seen to. After that, Walker would figure out a way to tell his senior officer what he really thought of him.

But that just made the long, silent trip toward the *Black Anchor* feel even longer.

INTEL

DECRYPTING

12345

COM CHATTER

- M4 CARBINE - short and light selective-fire assault rifle
- MERCENARY - paid-for-hire soldier
- SONAR - method of identifying objects underwater that uses echolocation
- SUPPRESSOR - device attached to a firearm that reduces the amount of noise and muzzle flash when fired

3245.98 ● ● ●

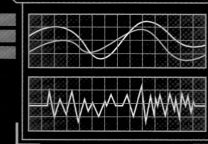

CHAPTER TWO

INFILTRATION

Deep under the surface, the SDV glided through the water carrying its six combat swimmers. Chief Walker piloted the vehicle while Cross sat beside him, navigating by GPS and SONAR. The instruments gave off the only visible light.

In the rear compartment sat Staff Sergeant Brighton, Second Lieutenant Larssen, Lieutenant Yamashita, and Hospital Corpsman Second Class Kyle Williams. All six men sat in nearly total darkness, breathing on regulators attached to the SDV's onboard air tanks.

An SDV insertion wasn't ideal for an assault on a gas-and-oil platform. Fast-roping down from a hovering helicopter would have suited better. But stealth was a much higher priority this time out than speed.

It wasn't so much the hostiles the team had to worry about as much as the Cuban patrol boats around the *Black Anchor*. If one of those crafts spotted them sneaking in, they might assume the wrong thing — that the US government was trying to sneak out the Hardwall mercenaries. That would almost certainly lead to hostility.

So the team chose the SDV approach, which filled Chief Walker with quiet satisfaction. Cross had initially argued for a fast-rope in, then for the Zodiac, almost as if he were afraid of using an SDV.

Patiently, and with respect, Walker had poked holes in each of Cross's suggestions for insertion until the SDV was the only option left. To be fair, Cross was qualified for SDV operations and he was a skilled navigator. However, Walker couldn't help but assume the lieutenant commander beside him was squirming with discomfort the whole time. And considering how far away in US waters they'd had to launch the SDV to avoid detection, it was an awful long time indeed.

Eventually, the *Black Anchor* platform showed up on the instruments. Walker maneuvered over to it. With practicied precision, he brought the SDV alongside the submerged structure. Then he cut the engines.

Walker nodded to Cross. Cross killed the instrumentation lights and hit the release to open the doors. The pair of them switched from the SDV's air supply to their own rebreathers. Then, still deep beneath the surface of the water, they exited the vehicle together.

Behind them, Brighton, Larssen, Yamashita, and Williams emerged. While Cross moored the SDV to the *Black Anchor*, the others glided over to the side of the spar and gently kick-stroked upward alongside it, taking great care to ascend slowly and silently.

Large blue and white LEDs dotted the outside of the tubes. They provided just enough illumination in the nighttime sea to lend the entire platform an alien appearance. Staring up at the overwhelming size of the rig, Walker could find no better word for it than *amazing*.

The underside of the *Black Anchor* consisted of six sealed vertical tubes wound around a seventh center tube. The tubes were hollow and allowed the rig to float or sink, depending on when the crew flushed or filled them with sea water.

Walker glanced at the set of four thick anchor chains that extended out into the darkness. It appeared that the crew had not been given a chance to extend the platform's drilling apparatus before the Hardwall mercenaries arrived.

Lieutenant Commander Cross quickly secured the SDV and signaled to Walker that it was time to go.

The pair of them followed the other four men up. They rose together at a leisurely pace so they didn't decompress too quickly. If they didn't pace themselves, then nitrogen bubbles would expand rapidly in their bloodstream, giving them decompression sickness. That would bring a quick end to the mission — and probably their lives.

Fortunately, the sea was relatively calm, so they didn't have to fight strong currents to stay on course.

As they neared the surface, they found steel emergency ladders running up the outside of the tubes. Cross took the lead, swimming over to the nearest ladder. He ascended to just below the surface of the water, then stopped to look back at his men. They spread out below Cross so they could all see him. Walker could practically feel their excitement electrifying the water around them.

Cross's first signal was for total noise discipline. It was pointless underwater, but vital topside. If they lost the element of surprise against the mercenary hostiles, the hostages would likely be the ones to suffer for it.

Next Cross set the climbing order. He would go first, followed by Walker, Brighton, Yamashita, then Williams. Larssen would take the rear.

When the swimmers finished shuffling their positions in the water, Cross held up one hand as if he were holding an invisible tennis ball. It wasn't a standard military hand signal, but a reminder of a certain point Cross had relentlessly driven into their heads throughout training: *think spherically.*

It was a vital concept, especially on a structure like this. Incoming attacks wouldn't be restricted to just the front and rear as on a normal battlefield. On this rig, with so many levels, enemies could just as easily attack from above or below, so the men had to be ready for trouble to come at them from every direction. Spherically.

Cross had repeated the concept constantly in training, making the hand signal every single time. *Think spherically, think spherically, think spherically.* It was solid advice, even if the repetition had gotten on Walker's nerves long ago.

Finally, Cross nodded to his men, looped an elbow around the ladder, and begin to remove his diving fins. The other five soldiers got in order below and did likewise, tucking the fins behind their backs under the straps holding on their small complement of gear. When his booted feet were free, Cross began the long climb upward. The squad followed.

When Walker broke the surface, his sense of weight suddenly returned, as if he were an astronaut coming back from a long journey in space. Now he felt every pound of his gear, though he tried not to let it slow him down. A stiff breeze chilled the water on his hands and face, and the gentle muffling of sound beneath the waves was replaced by the harsh splash and crash of the waves below.

Under the full moon's light, Walker could now see much farther. The improved view showed him the Cuban patrol boats waiting in the distance for their chance to close in and turn this mission into a total mess.

Cuba's naval fleet wasn't all that impressive compared to America's modern ships, but could still do plenty of damage. Intel told them that at least one Chinese vessel was nearby as well, though Walker couldn't see well enough to pick it out. But he did identify the mercenaries' boat moored on the other side of the platform.

If things went according to plan, it wouldn't matter how many boats were out on the water, or where they were located. But Walker knew that few plans remained intact after first contact with the enemy. Adaptation was almost a certainty in missions. Van Sant's men could certainly testify to that — that is, if they hadn't come planning to take hostages in the first place.

After a short climb, Cross reached the top of the ladder, coming to the underside of a metal catwalk. He suddenly gave the stop signal, and Walker passed it down even though he wasn't sure what the holdup was. He got his answer a moment later. A mercenary strolled by on a long, lonely patrol of the catwalk.

This particular metal walkway was the lowest level on the platform that was still above water. The single sentry had likely been stationed down here to watch for boats trying to sneak people on board.

Walker smiled. Cross had to realize that if he'd had his way and inserted via Zodiac instead of SDV, this sentry would have seen them and raised the alarm. Or worse, the mercs would have waited until they boarded and then cut them down on the ladder as they climbed up.

But because they'd done things Walker's way instead of Cross's, the team had remained undetected. They also gained the safety of the shadows beneath the walkway.

The sentry wore black fatigues, combat boots, and a Bluetooth earpiece. Slung around his shoulder was a Heckler & Koch MP5A3 submachine gun. A ballistic vest covered his broad chest. As he paced, his eyes remained focused on the thrashing waters below, hoping to spot and prevent any attempted insertions — like the one Shadow Squadron had just successfully performed.

The sentry continued his circuit, passing by the ladder where Cross's team waited below. He was entirely unaware of their presence. As the sentry passed, Cross signaled to Walker.

Quietly, Cross snuck up behind the mercenary with Walker on his heels. As soon as they reached the walkway, Cross rushed up behind the guard and slapped a choke hold around his neck. Cross's muscles tightened. He squeezed the man's windpipe and pulsing arteries closed.

Cross pulled the sentry to his knees, his weight pulling the man backward. The mercenary tried to reach for his submachine gun hanging around his shoulder.

SLIT!

Walker cut the gun strap using his knife, and took the weapon from the merc. He casually pitched it over the side of the safety rail and into the ocean.

Unable to shout for help, and growing weaker from the lack of blood flow to his brain, the sentry flailed wildly. He clawed at Cross's forearm. Cross took the blows, patiently waiting for the sentry to slip into unconsciousness.

The mercenary went for his boot knife, but Walker snatched the weapon away before he could reach it. Finally, the merc's eyes slowly slipped shut and he slumped into Cross's arms.

Cross carefully laid him on the catwalk. He checked his pulse, then nodded. With Walker's help, Cross flipped the merc over onto his belly.

Walker kept a lookout while Cross produced a pair of plastic zip ties from his pocket.

ZIP!

ZIP!

Walker secured the man's hands behind his back. After that, he secured one ankle to the metal walkway rail. A quick search revealed the man had no other weapons or ID of any sort.

Walker pitched the man's knife into the churning waters below, then did the same with the man's Bluetooth headset. Only then did he signal for the rest of the team to come up the ladder to the walkway.

Brighton, Yamashita, Williams, and Larssen took their positions. Williams checked the downed mercenary. He was alive but deeply unconscious. Willaims nodded once to Cross.

The six of them then spent a moment pocketing their swimming gear and readying their weapons. Each of them was armed with a suppressor-equipped

M4 carbine with a modified, shorter barrel for the inevitable close-quarters combat that this mission would require.

Staff Sergeant Brighton had complained about that during the mission briefing, clearly hoping to use his prized AA-12 combat shotgun aboard the *Black Anchor*. However, Cross had accurately pointed out that the AA-12 just put too much lead into the air for this mission. And it was anything but precise — even if Brighton argued otherwise. Which he had. Repeatedly.

When everyone was ready, Cross gathered the squad and addressed them once more without words. He held up five fingers, reminding them of the number of hostile targets remaining onboard.

The Cubans' intelligence suggested that only six Hardwall mercenaries had gotten off their boat and subdued the oil platform's crew. Presumably, all five of the remaining mercs were armed and armored similarly to the sentry they'd just incapacicated. And they were sure to be in contact with each other via their headsets.

Cross tapped his watch, indicating it was only a matter of time before the other mercs noticed the missing man was no longer keeping in contact.

That meant Shadow Squadron would have to move fast. And quietly.

According to the Cubans' intelligence, the Hardwall men were keeping the hostages near the helipad.

Cross circled one finger in the air, mimicking a helicopter's spinning propeller. The message was clear: reaching the helipad was their first priority.

Walker knew this without having to read hand signals. Freeing the hostages was the utmost of importance on any mission. Engaging hostiles before securing the hostages almost always led to the loss of life.

Finally, Cross held up the *think spherically* signal one more time. As one, the men each gave a sharp nod.

Together, they moved out along the catwalk to a set of stairs farther on. Their eyes — and the muzzles of their carbines — kept in constant motion, scanning for trouble from all directions. Up, down, left, right — the enemies could come from anywhere here.

It didn't take Shadow Squadron long to find the trouble they went looking for.

INTEL

DECRYPTING

12345

COM CHATTER

- BALLISTIC VEST - bulletproof piece of armor worn across the torso
- CANALPHONE - headphones that fit inside the canal of the ear
- MP5 - German-made, 9mm submachine gun
- SEAHAWK - helicopter designed specifically for traveling over water

3245.98 ● ● ●

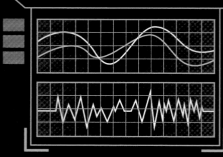

CHAPTER THREE

ASSAULT

The stairs up from the lower catwalk led up to the center of the structure where they found a nexus of stairways, ladders, and walkways. It resembled a spider's nest made of metal. An array of dim LEDs created a creepy web of intersecting shadows and dark spaces where enemies could hide.

Walker strained his ears listening for any sound of approaching mercenaries. He peered around, finding the stairs and walkways all labeled in Chinese. That wasn't a problem for him, since he was fluent, but he saw confusion on his teammates' faces.

Walker pointed out two separate paths that would take the team to the helipad. Cross gave a quick grateful nod and split the cell into two fireteams. He took Yamashita and Williams in one direction and Walker led Brighton and Larssen in the other. Walker's men crossed the underside of the helipad to a metal ladder on the far side. The three of them climbed until Walker reached the top and stopped. Carefully, he peered over the edge to take stock of the situation.

Twenty or so miserable-looking Chinese and Cuban hostages sat huddled in the center of the helipad. They were leaning against each other for warmth, or shivering with their arms wrapped around themselves. None of them spoke to each other or to their captors. To Walker's eyes, none of them appeared to be injured or otherwise suffering, but it would be Williams's job to say for sure.

Walker scanned for mercenaries. Two of them had been left to guard the hostages. Like the man down on the catwalk, the guards wore ballistic vests and carried submachine guns. One of them stood at the edge of the helipad looking out over the ocean, holding a writhing, pitiful Chinese crewman by his neck. The other guard stood by the group of hostages in the center. The second guard was laughing as the hostage in the mercenary's grasp squirmed.

"What's the matter?" the mercenary demanded of his terrified prisoner. "Don't have to use the bathroom anymore? Don't be shy, we're all guys here. Go ahead, do your business."

Walker clenched his teeth. He had to struggle to repress the urge to aim his M4 one-handed and drop the thug where he stood. Yet, as satisfying as that might be, he couldn't be sure that the man wouldn't knock the prisoner overboard. And Walker didn't want to get into the habit of shooting people just because they were bullies.

CLICK-A-CLICK. The waterproof canalphone in Walker's right ear activated. Walker scanned across the helipad for Lieutenant Commander Cross's fireteam. He could just make out Cross crouching at the top of the stairway leading onto the helipad on the other side of the platform.

Walker tapped his canalphone twice, returning Cross's signal. Cross took aim at the mercenary closest to himself who was standing near the bulk of the hostages. Walker tensed on the ladder, preparing to move on the hostile who was harassing the captured crewman. He glanced back at Brighton, and held up three fingers. Then two. Then one . . .

The men launched into action, performing a variation on a set of maneuvers they had practiced many times in training. Cross stood up into full view of both guards and actually whistled to get their attention. It was just the kind of grandstanding that Walker found most annoying about Cross. However, it was undeniably effective: both guards turned to look at Cross in stunned surprise. That was when Walker mounted the helipad deck from the ladder.

Cross fired a single round.

BANG!

The guard folded up in the middle and sank to his knees. The hostages scrambled back away from him, parting for Cross as he rushed over to the downed mercenary.

A moment after Cross fired, the Hardwall mercenary by the edge of the helipad reacted with predictable cowardice. He yanked his gasping Chinese prisoner around in a half circle and clutched him from behind as a human shield. The mercenary brought his submachine gun up one-handed over the hostage's shoulder and pointed it at Cross.

Walker momentarily considered blasting the submachine gun out of the mercenary's hand. Instead, he aimed down at the mercenary's right thigh.

POP!

The bullet drilled right through his leg. The mercenary yelped and collapsed as his leg buckled, giving his human shield a chance to dash over to his huddled coworkers.

That's good at least, Walker reflected. However, the wounded mercenary was aware of him now, and he was still perfectly capable of firing his weapon. As the merc flopped onto his back, he started to raise his gun with one hand.

"Drop it!" Walker demanded, reluctant to shoot an American citizen. "Now!"

Whether the man would have complied or not, Walker would never know. No sooner had Walker shouted his warning when Lieutenant Commander Cross raised his M4 and put the issue to rest, squeezing off a shot that caught the mercenary's MP5 right above the trigger.

KARRRANG!

Hot metal shrapnel burst from the weapon as it flew out of the man's hand. When the ruined submachine gun clattered to the deck, Cross shot it again.

KACHUNK!

The weapon skittered over the side of the helipad and into the ocean.

Walker glanced at Cross, glaring at the man who'd potentially just saved his life. Cross flicked Walker a salute and a smirk. Walker just shook his head and turned away. He wasn't going to begrudge Cross for taking the shot, but did the man have to show off when he did it?

Brighton and Larssen had climbed up onto the helipad behind Walker. They moved past him to zip-cuff the wounded mercenary. They pulled off his Bluetooth headset, bound his hands behind his back, and then treated his nonfatal leg wound. Walker let the man lie and joined Cross. The lieutenant commander was just finishing zip-cuffing the other mercenary. The Hardwall man lay on his stomach gasping for air, trying to recover from being struck by Cross's first shot. The bullet had been stopped by the ballistic vest, sparing his life, but knocking the wind out of him.

The stunned hostages milled around, staring at the American soldiers with every imaginable variety of dumbfounded shock. Two bullets, two incapacitated guards, no deaths. Walker had to admit that Cross did well. Really well.

Cross looked over at Walker and mouthed the word, "Clear?" Walker nodded. Williams came over at the same time, leaving Yamashita to keep a lookout for the rest of the hostiles. For the moment, none of the three remaining Hardwall mercs were anywhere to be seen. So Williams walked among the skittish hostages, looking for obvious signs of trauma and asking quiet questions.

Walker approached the hostage whom the second mercenary had tried to use as a human shield. "Are you hurt?" he whispered in Chinese.

The hostage's glassy, confused eyes slowly came back into focus. He shook his head. "They didn't hurt us," the man said in a soft, breathless voice.

"Do you know how many guards are left?" Walker asked.

"Four," the hostage answered. "One is on the catwalk below."

Walker nodded. That one was no longer a problem. "Where are the rest?" he asked.

"Operations control, with the station chief," the hostage said, pointing up toward the highest point of the facility. "They're talking to my government."

Walker relayed that information to Cross. The lieutenant commander stood as Brighton and Larssen dragged the wounded mercenary over to them. The hostages backed off again. The mercenary moaned and tried to clutch at his leg with his zip-cuffed hands, cursing and yelling at them.

"Can we give this guy something to shut him up?" Brighton whispered in annoyance to Cross and Williams. "He's going to give our position away."

"I've got something for him," Cross said, stepping next to the wounded man. The mercenary looked up as he Cross slammed the butt of his carbine square into the merc's forehead. The man fell flat on his back, and his head bounced off the deck. He lost consciousness instantly.

"Oh!" Brighton said, flinching and hiding his mouth behind his hand. Then, with a huge grin, he crouched over the unconscious mercenary. "You all right, man?" Brighton joked. "Walk it off, buddy."

"Shh!" Walker hissed, giving Brighton the noise-discipline signal. The combat controller snapped back to his feet, his face turning red.

"All right, form up," Cross said softly, calling his men together. "We've got three hostiles remaining. They are in or around the op center at the top of the facility." He addressed Williams. "Stay and give the hostages a once-over." Then he looked at Larssen. "Watch his back, and keep an eye on the injured mercenaries."

"Sir," Williams and Larssen said together.

"You three are with me," Cross said to Walker, Yamashita, and Brighton. "Let's go sew this one up."

"Sir," Yamashita and Brighton said. Walker only gave a curt nod.

The fireteam joined the lieutenant commander and left the helipad. With eyes and gun barrels sweeping back and forth and up and down, the men moved up a metal stairway to the platform's upper levels. The stairway wrapped around the outside of the platform and led into a narrow exterior walkway with pipes, valves, and gauges on both sides.

From there, the team passed through a wire-strewn computer center, a sparse recreation room with a television and ping-pong table, and the kitchen and dining area. Each room was messy and cluttered, evidence suggesting that the Hardwall men had rousted the crew in the middle of the workday. But there was no sign of more hostiles.

After clearing the rooms on that level, the team emerged onto another walkway. It wrapped around the other side of the structure, leading to another stairway to the topmost levels. Before the fireteam reached the stairs, Cross suddenly gave the stop signal. He looked over the rail at the helipad below. Walker looked down as well, trying to figure out what had caught the lieutenant commander's attention.

Walker saw that the hostages had grouped up at the edge of the helipad closest to the center of the platform. Williams moved among them, making sure everyone was in good health. Larssen was finishing zip-cuffing the two mercenaries to a stair railing. Faint smears of blood shone in the lights, indicating where Larssen had dragged the unconscious, wounded mercenary over to the rail.

"Lieutenants," Cross breathed, tapping his canalphone. "Did either of you call for medical evac?"

"Negative," Larssen and Williams both answered, confusion evident in their voices.

Walker shared their confusion for a moment until he heard what Cross had already noticed: the sound of helicopter blades chopping through the night air. The Navy had a Seahawk chopper on standby in case of emergencies. But this incoming helicopter didn't sound like a Seahawk, and it wasn't coming from the right direction.

All too quickly, the aircraft roared up out of the darkness. It threw blinding halogen spotlights onto the helipad. One light played over the frightened hostages. The other spotlight illuminated Larssen, who was just crossing the helipad to rejoin Williams.

Cross and Walker both recognized the make of the helicopter as it rose into view. It was a Russian-made Mil Mi-8 — a troop transport and fast-attack gunship employed by both the Chinese and the Cuban militaries. The hostages' countrymen had come to rescue them at last. And now, in a huddled mass of terrified hostages, they had spotted an armed soldier standing over them.

The chopper turned its broadside toward the landing pad. A door in the side slid open. "Get out of there!" Walker and Cross called, hitting their canalphones simultaneously. Their warning was too late.

RAT-A-TAT-TAT-TAT-TAT-TAT-TAT-TAT!
RAT-A-TAT-TAT-TAT-TAT-TAT-TAT-TAT!

Machine guns flared to life as bullets drew a crisscrossing line across the concrete right toward Larssen. He had already started running away from the hostages and toward cover, but he wasn't fast enough. Larssen's body jerked, spun, and fell — all in the blink of an eye. He landed only a few yards short of safety. The helicopter lowered toward the pad, preparing to offload soldiers.

Cross pointed toward the helicopter. "Yamashita," he said through clenched teeth. "Tail rotor."

"Sir," Yamashita said without a hint of emotion in his voice.

As one, Yamashita and Cross raised their weapons and fired in the helicopter's direction.

POP!

POP!

POP!

Walker had to admit his commanding officer was one of the best shots he had ever seen. The lieutenant commander managed to squeeze off two three-round bursts that dug into the helicopter's hull just below were the spinning main rotor. A third burst followed, raising a thick plume of white smoke.

SKREEEEEEEEEEEEEE!

The helicopter's engine squealed like a wounded animal.

As good a shot as Cross was, however, Yamashita was even better. Firing one bullet at a time, he punched a line of holes in the helicopter's narrow tail, damaging the mechanism of the stabilizing rotor on the rear.

The chopper bucked suddenly in the air. It swerved wildly to one side. The pilot fought the spin and just barely managed to keep it from slamming into the edge of the helipad and crashing into the ocean below.

Walker saw the gunmen inside clinging to the handholds for dear life. They were unable to even find where the shots were coming from, much less return fire.

"Cease fire," Cross ordered. He and Yamashita lowered their weapons.

Barely able to control the aircraft, the pilot veered away from the *Black Anchor* and raced back the way he'd come. The helicopter fishtailed across the sky like a car swerving on an icy road.

Walker assumed the craft had launched from one of the vessels keeping watch on the water. He wondered if it would be able to make it back and land in one piece.

"Williams!" Cross barked, pointing over the rail toward where Larssen lay bleeding. It was technically a breach of operational protocol to refer to any of the team members by name while engaged in the field, but Walker could hardly fault the slip.

"Got him," came Williams's response over the canalphone. The corpsman rushed across the helipad and crouched over Larssen. He broke out the first-aid kit he hadn't yet needed for the hostages. A moment later, Williams said, "He's alive, Commander — barely. We need our evac chopper."

Cross had already produced a waterproof radio

from one of his cargo pockets. He keyed in the emergency frequency. "Angel, this is Preacher," he called, concealing the distress in his voice. "Man down. We need an airlift."

"Preacher, this is Angel," the pilot of the standby chopper called back. "Roger that, Preacher. ETA is five minutes."

Cross signed off. Then he tapped his canalphone and said, "Five minutes, Williams."

Williams sighed. "Sir."

"I'll gather our dive gear," Brighton said, turning as if to head back down below.

"Leave it," Cross said, stowing the radio. "You heard the man, we've only got five minutes."

"Sir?" Brighton said.

"Three hostiles left," Cross said, "and one hostage."

The distress from seeing Larssen down, and possibly dying, was absent from Cross's face now. In its place was a cold, grim anger. "Let's move," he barked.

"What about the SDV?" Brighton asked.

"The Navy can send a SEAL team if they want it back," Cross replied. "Now move out."

Brighton opened his mouth to say something else, but was silenced by the chattering of submachine gun fire.

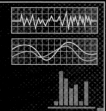

INTEL

DECRYPTING

||||||||| ||||||||||| |||||

12345

COM CHATTER

- CROSSFIRE – lines of fire that overlap each other
- FIRETEAM – a small unit of soldiers
- M84 FLASHBANG – a nonlethal grenade that temporarily deafens and blinds those caught in its blast
- SUPPRESSING FIRE – gunfire used to render a target temporarily ineffective or unusable

3245.98 ● ● ●

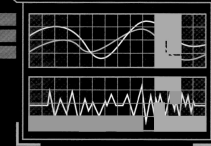

CHAPTER FOUR

FIREFIGHT

Bullets roared from ahead and above, ringing off the walls, and the metal catwalk. Walker saw where the shots came from and realized what must have happened. The hostiles, unaware of Shadow Squadron's arrival, had heard the chopper open fire. The sudden departure of the helicopter had undoubtedly surprised them, but now they'd spotted Cross's fireteam, realizing they were still under siege. Fortunately, rather than move in for the kill or spread out to coordinate a crossfire, they'd simply opened fire from where they stood.

Two mercenaries were shooting from the catwalk one level up. Most of their shots were wild and

panicked, though one glanced off Cross's helmet and another grazed Brighton across the shoulder blade.

The fireteam immediately took cover. Walker had the clearest line of sight on the gunmen. He threw a line of fire up toward them, sending them diving backward for cover.

Cross angrily signaled the team to move up and take the stairway, unwilling to let up on the mercenaries now that they'd engaged. Walker laid down cover fire to keep the mercenaries' heads down.

RAT-A-TAT-TAT!

Hissing in pain from the wound on his back, Brighton rushed to a position at the foot of the steps and fired a few rounds up over the men's heads. Yamashita backtracked and scrambled up a ladder, looking for a level field of fire. One of the mercenaries saw him climbing and fired off what was left in his clip, but Walker drove him back with another stream of suppressing fire. The other mercenary fired back, forcing Yamashita to roll around a corner, and kept his head down.

For a moment, no one moved and no one fired. The Hardwall men couldn't come down, and Yamashita had a firing line on their only avenue of escape. However, the mercs had clear lanes of fire on the only route the fireteam could take to reach them.

They were at a stalemate. Time was running out.

Suddenly, Lieutenant Commander Cross stood up. With his back to a wall, he moved toward a position directly beneath where the two mercenaries were holed up together. Then he signaled Walker to join Brighton at the base of the stairs and for the two of them to get ready to move.

Walker frowned. Yamashita wasn't in a position to provide covering fire. He only had a line on the mercenaries' escape route. If Brighton and Walker went up the stairs, the mercenaries would have a nice, narrow lane of fire to cut them down.

What is Cross thinking? Walker wondered.

Reading the expression on Walker's face, Cross winked, then gave him the think spherically sign. He reached into his belt and drew an M84 flashbang grenade, then nodded at the walkway overhead.

Walker still wasn't sure exactly what Cross had in mind, but he got ready to move just the same. Cross pulled the pin, but held the spoon and started counting down from five on his free hand. At two, he let go of the spoon but held onto the grenade, letting its fuse cook off in his hand. At zero, he signaled for Walker and Brighton to go, and the two men immediately rushed up the stairs together, staring down the long stretch of walkway between themselves and the mercs.

Hearing their approach, the mercs leaned around with their weapons. At the same moment, Cross took one step out from under the catwalk and threw his flashbang straight up in the air. It popped up over the rail right next to the mercenaries' boots.

POP!

The flare and the concussion knocked the mercs off their feet, giving Walker and Brighton all the time they needed to close in and disarm them.

Cross and Yamashita quickly joined them. Walker signaled for Brighton to keep an eye out for the last mercenary. Then Walker went to work zip-cuffing the mercenaries to the catwalk.

With that done, Walker pulled out both men's Bluetooth headsets and put one to his left ear. Cross took the other one and did the same, signaling his fireteam to advance on the op center.

"What the heck is going on out there?!" the last remaining mercenary shouted through the earpiece. "Somebody answer me!"

"It's over," Cross said. "The rest of your men have been neutralized."

There was a long pause. Then a voice asked, "Who is this?"

To Walker, the mercenary sounded scared and angry — a dangerous combination.

"Give yourself up," Cross responded. "You've run out of time, and I lack patience to argue with you."

The mercenary let out a half-crazed cackle. "Oh, really?" he said. "Does that mean I should just kill my hostage, then?"

Cross frowned. Walker wondered if the lieutenant commander had forgotten there was one hostage left.

The fireteam made it to the last walkway that led to the operations command station. The station had a large window on the side, but the lights inside went out as the team approached. Cross signaled a halt in front of the one door that led inside.

"No answer to that, huh?" the mercenary said. Walker could hear a second person whimpering in the background whenever the man talked. Walker glanced at Cross, but the commander remained silent.

"I'll tell you what," the merc said. "Me and my new friend here are going to get on my boat and leave, and you're going to let us. If anybody tries to 'neutralize' me, I swear —"

"Forget it," Cross snapped.

"No?" the merc said. "Then come in here and get me. The second I hear running footsteps, I'm putting two bullets in the back of this guy's head and coming out with guns blazing."

Cross clenched his teeth. Then he closed his eyes and took a deep breath. He seemed to be considering daring the mercenary to do just that.

"Wait," Walker said, addressing both the mercenary and Cross. Walker held up a hand, silently urging Cross to give him a moment. Cross reluctantly nodded.

"Who's this now?" the mercenary demanded.

"Let me explain the situation to you," Walker said, his voice steady, and heavy with authority. "In two minutes, a helicopter's coming to pick us up. And we're all going to be on it because you can be sure that the Cubans are already on their way here to clean up this mess their own way."

"Wait," the mercenary said, his voice sounding rattled all of a sudden. "Who are you guys? Are you Americans? Did Van Sant send you?"

"You're running out of time," Walker said. "If you don't come out, we're just going to leave and let you have this conversation with the Cubans. And I promise you, if you kill that hostage, you're on your own."

"Hang on a second, I —" the merc began.

"It's now or never," Walker said, interrupting him. Walker held up the earpiece so the merc could hear the approaching chopper. "Our ride's here. What's it going to be?"

At first, nothing happened. Then, slowly, the mercenary opened the op center door and stepped out. He froze when he saw four M4 barrels pointing at him down the walkway.

"All right," he started to say. "Let's just —"

"Put your weapon down," Walker ordered him.

KLANK-KLANK!

The mercenary dropped his MP5 on the ground and put his hands up, uncertainty on his face. Cross dropped the Bluetooth headset and crunched it underfoot. He walked over to the mercenary.

"Kick the weapon over here," Walker said, coming up behind Cross. The mercenary slid the gun across the floor. Cross stepped over it, letting Walker catch it under one foot. "Now get —"

Williams's voice cut in on the team's canalphones. "Commander," the corpsman said, his voice somber. "Neil's . . . not going to make it."

Cross's face went dark. "What?" the mercenary asked, unable to hear the conversation but reacting to the sudden change in Cross's expression. "What's going on?"

Cross brought up his M4 and smashed the butt stock across the bridge of the mercenary's nose.

KRUNCH!!

The mercenary stumbled backward, bounced off the op center door and fell forward on his hands and knees. Cross placed his boot on the man's back, pressing him to the floor.

Walker came forward, planning to pull Cross back, but stopped when he saw the commander's rage had vanished. Without saying a word, Cross yanked the mercenary's arm up at an awkward angle and zip-cuffed it to the safety rail. Then he brushed past Walker, picked up the mercenary's MP5 and hurled it off the walkway. It clattered down through the superstructure and ended with a splash in the darkness.

"Move out!" Cross growled. He turned and walked back the way the fireteam had come, not bothering to check on the hostage in the op center or the bound mercenary whimpering at his feet.

Yamashita fell into step behind Cross without a word. Brighton and Walker hesitated a moment and exchanged a look.

"Yikes," Brighton said.

"Let's move," Walker said.

From the sound of it, the Seahawk helicopter was less than a minute out. *That means the Cubans are on their way,* Walker thought.

INTEL

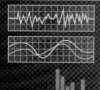

DECRYPTING

12345

COM CHATTER

- ARMY RANGER – elite soldiers who have graduated from Army Ranger school

- CREED – a saying, or a system of guideliness that an individual or group lives by

- ROGUE – if a soldier goes rogue, he or she acts independently and without the consent of his commanding officers

3245.98 ● ● ●

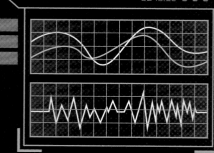

EVAC

The Seahawk was halfway home. Since the team had left the *Black Anchor*, Cross had sat in silence, staring down at the shrouded, lifeless form resting on the deck below him.

Second Lieutenant Neil Larssen had lived long enough to be brought onto the helicopter, but he'd died only a few minutes out over the water.

Walker had been trying without success to think of something to say to Cross that didn't sound forced. But no matter how hard he tried, he couldn't think of anything.

"We shouldn't have left them," Cross said. He looked up at Walker. "We should have brought all those Hardwall thugs back home with us to answer for what they did."

"That wasn't the mission," Walker said. "We had to do it this way so the Cubans could take credit for the rescue. Letting them save face is supposed to offset the damage Van Sant's people would've done to our country's reputation."

"But if we'd brought at least one back," Cross argued, "we could've had him give evidence against Van Sant and bring the whole organization down. But now all Van Sant has to do is claim they went rogue and condemn their actions. He'll probably get away with everything."

"He might try that," Walker admitted. "But even if he pulls it off, I think Hardwall Security is about to find itself on some government lists. You know, the kind that make it very hard to find good work."

"Maybe," Cross said. He sighed. "What a mess. This whole thing is going to be a diplomatic nightmare."

"Let the State Department worry about that," Walker said. "Just remember that for your part, you did everything right."

"Not everything," Cross said quietly. His eyes went back to the body at his feet.

"That wasn't your fault," Walker said.

"'The lives of my teammates and the success of our mission depend on me,'" Cross said, quoting from the US Navy SEAL creed.

"'In the worst of conditions,'" Walker said, quoting a different section, "'the legacy of my teammates steadies my resolve and silently guides my every deed.'"

"'I will draw on every remaining ounce of strength to protect my teammates,'" Cross countered. "I didn't protect him, did I?"

"Knowing full well the hazards of my profession, I will always strive to uphold the prestige, honor, and esprit de corps of my regiment," Walker said.

Cross raised an eyebrow, though he didn't lift his gaze. "What's that from?"

"The Ranger creed," Walker explained. "I'm not sure that's exactly how it goes, but that's the general idea behind it. Neil was a Ranger . . . wouldn't you say he lived up to that standard?"

"Always," Cross said.

"Then mourn him, and honor him," Walker said. "But don't make his loss about yourself. If you start down that road, you'll end up feeling guilty whenever you look around and don't see him. Trust me: I've been right where you are now."

Cross was quiet for a long while, apparently considering the chief's words.

Bit by bit, Cross seemed to relax a little. He looked up. "Does that mean we actually have a second thing in common with each other, Chief Walker?" he asked.

"Something else?" Walker asked. "What was the first thing?"

"The fact that we're both SEALs, of course," Cross said.

Walker smirked.

"Well, don't get ahead of yourself, Commander," Walker deadpanned. "I'm an *SDV* SEAL after all . . ."

Cross grinned. "Right, Chief." He took a slow, deep breath. "And thanks."

Walker nodded. "Sir."

MISSION DEBRIEFING

OPERATION

BLACK ANCHOR 1234

PRIMARY OBJECTIVE

- Secure the oil rig platform and transport hostages to safety

SECONDARY OBJECTIVES

- Minimize damage done to Hardwall mercenaries

x Avoid contact with the Cuban and Chinese forces

STATUS

2/3 COMPLETE

3245.98 ● ● ●

WALKER, ALONSO

RANK: Chief Petty Officer
BRANCH: Navy SEAL
PSYCH PROFILE: Walker is Shadow Squadron's second-in-command. His combat experience, skepticism, and distrustful nature make him a good counter-balance to Cross's command.

I had to reprimand the other members of Shadow Sqadron for neglecting to file their *Black Anchor* debriefings in a timely manner. But overall, they performed admirably in the field. All the hostages were recovered unharmed, and the men kept their emotions under control even when one of our own was shot down. Cross was really shaken up over losing Larssen. We all were. But we were able to keep it together and complete the mission.

Second Lieutenant Neil Larssen was a good man, and a good soldier. He will be missed.

— Chief Petty Officer Alonso Walker

ERROR

UNAUTHORIZED

USER MUST HAVE LEVEL 12 CLEARANCE
OR HIGHER IN ORDER TO GAIN ACCESS
TO FURTHER MISSION INFORMATION.

2019.681

CARL BOWEN

Carl Bowen is a father, husband, and writer living in Lawrenceville, Georgia. He was born in Louisiana, lived briefly in England, and was raised in Georgia where he went to school. He has published a handful of novels, short stories, and comics. For Stone Arch Books, he has retold *20,000 Leagues Under the Sea*, *The Strange Case of Dr. Jekyll and Mr. Hyde*, *The Jungle Book*, *Aladdin and the Magic Lamp*, *Julius Caesar*, and *The Murders in the Rue Morgue*. He is the original author of *BMX Breakthrough* as well as the Shadow Squadron series.

INTEL

DECRYPTING

LOADING...

ARTIST

WILSON TORTOSA

Wilson "Wunan" Tortosa is a Filipino comic book artist best known for his works on *Tomb Raider* and the American relaunch of *Battle of the Planets* for Top Cow Productions. Wilson attended Philippine Cultural High School, then went on to the University of Santo Tomas, where he graduated with a Bachelor's Degree in Fine Arts, majoring in Advertising.

COLORIST

BENNY FUENTES

Benny Fuentes lives in Villahermosa, Tabasco, in Mexico, where the temperature is just as hot as the sauce. He studied graphic design in college, but now he works as a full-time colorist in the comic book and graphic novel industry for companies like Marvel, DC Comics, and Top Cow Productions. He shares his home with two crazy cats, Chelo and Kitty, who act like they own the place.

2019.681

CLASSIFIED

AUTHOR DEBRIEFING

CARL BOWEN

Q/When and why did you decide to become a writer?
A/I've enjoyed writing ever since I was in elementary school. I wrote as much as I could, hoping to become the next Lloyd Alexander or Stephen King, but I didn't sell my first story until I was in college. It had been a long wait, but the day I saw my story in print was one of the best days of my life.

Q/What made you decide to write *Shadow Squadron*?
A/As a kid, my heroes were always brave knights or noble loners who fought because it was their duty, not for fame or glory. I think the special ops soldiers of the US military embody those ideals. Their jobs are difficult and often thankless, so I wanted to show how cool their jobs are, but also express my gratitude for our brave warriors.

Q/What inspires you to write?
A/My biggest inspiration is my family. My wife's love and support lifts me up when this job seems too hard to keep going. My son is another big inspiration.

He's three years old, and I want him to read my books and feel the same way I did when I read my favorite books as a kid. And if he happens to grow up to become an elite soldier in the US military, that would be pretty awesome, too.

Q/Describe what it was like to write these books.

A/The only military experience I have is a year I spent in the Army ROTC. It gave me a great respect for the military and its soldiers, but I quickly realized I would have made a pretty awful soldier. I recently got to test out a friend's arsenal of firearms, including a combat shotgun, an AR-15 rifle, and a Barrett M82 sniper rifle. We got to blow apart an old fax machine.

Q/What is your favorite book, movie, and game?

A/My favorite book of all time is *Don Quixote*. It's crazy and it makes me laugh. My favorite movie is either *Casablanca* or *Double Indemnity*, old black-and-white movies made before I was born. My favorite game, hands down, is *Skyrim*, in which you play a heroic dragonslayer. But not even *Skyrim* can keep me from writing more *Shadow Squadron* stories, so you won't have to wait long to read more about Ryan Cross and his team. That's a promise.

INTEL

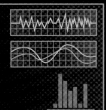

DECRYPTING
‖‖‖‖‖‖‖   ‖‖‖‖‖‖‖‖‖‖ ‖‖‖ |

12345

COM CHATTER

-MISSION PREVIEW: EAGLE DOWN
A Colombian drug network, or nexus, is shipping illegal drugs onto US soil via submersible vessels from somewhere in the Colombian jungle. With the local military's assistance, Staff Sergeant Edgar Brighton will infiltrate the jungle, locate the shipyard, and call in coordinates for a precision airstrike.

3245.98 ● ● ●

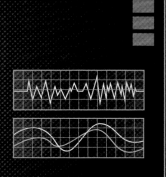

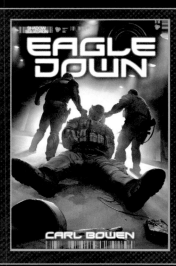

EAGLE DOWN

Just before dawn, the pilot said over the intercom that the plane was over the jump zone. Brighton donned his night-vision mask, then stepped up to the Cessna's side door beside the jumpmaster. With the mask's four 16mm intensifier tubes sticking out like fingers around his eyes, it gave Brighton an eerie, insect-like appearance. Brighton saw the jumpmaster do a double take as he approached.

Strange looks aside, Brighton preferred the expanded field of view of his panoramic mask to the ones the rest of Shadow Squadron used. The others made him feel like his field of vision was limited.

Following the jumpmaster's pointed finger, Brighton located a tiny clearing a few hundred yards from the bank of the muddy river below. From its center, a small infrared beacon blinked. That was the signal the Colombians' advance team had set up to guide Brighton to them. Thankfully, it was visible only via night-vision equipment from above. Brighton didn't want to land amidst armed hostiles.

Clearing his thoughts, Brighton readied himself to jump. From this height, it was going to be tricky hitting the bull's-eye on the clearing, but he wasn't worried. A pre-dawn precision jump into heavy jungle was nothing compared to having to deal with drug-dealing guerillas shooting at you. So, with a well-trained and fully confident mind, he awaited the jumpmaster's signal.

"GO!" the jumpmaster yelled. A moment later, Brighton hurled himself out the door and into the darkness.

The elation of his first few seconds of free fall made Brighton's head swim. Skydiving had always thrilled him, ever since his first tandem jump with his father at age 15. He loved to let the thrill of the descent fill his mind as the Earth soared up toward him.

But this time, Brighton allowed himself only a few fleeting moments of joy before he let his training

take over. Then he spread his arms and legs to right himself in the air and maximize wind resistance. Brighton checked the altimeter and GPS device mounted on his wrist, then he shifted in the air until he located the target beacon with his goggles once more.

The easy, gradual turn gave him a good opportunity to observe the lay of the land. With his eyes, he traced the many river inlets and outlets, memorizing the few landmarks he could make out with his night vision. When he was low enough, he opened his chute.

Brighton bent himself into a wide downward spiral. He was confident that would put him within ten yards of the clearing, if not dead center. Easily, in fact.

The tricky part, however, was the actual landing. All of Brighton's gear made him heavy under the chute. As expected, Brighton managed to hole-in-one the small clearing. But when he hit the muddy ground, the extra weight made him stumble. A gust of wind pushed his chute into the branches overhead. Brighton was forced to leave it dangling for a moment to set down his secondary pack, then squirmed out of his rigging.

Standard procedure was to bury his jump gear after landing in order to minimize the chances that enemy forces would discover his intrusion. He had just opened his pack to grab his shovel when he heard several pairs of boots squelching through the mud.

Brighton saw a group of eight men in old-school camouflage uniforms emerge from the jungle shadows. They were rugged, hard-looking men. To Brighton, they looked more like hardened special forces than policemen. And they all looked like they were quite a bit older than Brighton, although that could just be due to the wear and tear of years of combat experience.

"Hey, fellas," Brighton greeted them in Spanish. "Could you have picked a smaller clearing for my landing? I could almost see this one from the sky."

"You're the one Gaitan sent?" the one closest to Brighton asked in a gravelly voice.

Brighton nodded. The man said nothing, but instead signaled to another soldier behind Brighton's back.

"Give me a sec to set up my radio," Brighton said. "If one of you could pull that chute down and bury it for me, I'd appreciate it."

Brighton knelt beside his pack. He'd just opened the waterproof flap and turned up the whip antenna when a man came up behind him. Without thinking, Brighton handed the folded-up shovel over his shoulder.

"Here you go," Brighton said. "I appreciate the help —"

ZIRRRRRRT!

Fifty thousand volts of electricity poured into Brighton from between his shoulder blades. Every nerve and muscle in his body blazed with pain.

He collapsed in a heap. Brighton felt like he had no control over his own body. He had endured this exact sensation before during his training. Otherwise, he wouldn't have even known what had just happened.

In the back of his mind, far from the pain, Brighton understood he'd been zapped with a stun gun. No sooner had Brighton come to this realization when he received another jolt.

ZIRRRRRRT!

Brighton tried to yell, but his mouth wouldn't open. His teeth were clenched shut due to the muscles spasming through his entire body.

While Brighton lay gasping, one of the Colombians turned him over on his back. The rest of soldiers gathered around to look at him. One of them held the flashing IR beacon in his hand. At this close range, its intense glare stung Brighton's eyes through his night-vision mask.

A man knelt in front of him. He held the stun gun up where Brighton could see it. "He's still conscious," the man said, sneering. He lowered the stun gun toward Brighton again.

It's not a knockout wand, man, Brighton wanted to say. But he was in too much pain to move, let alone speak.

Fortunately, one of the other soldiers grabbed the stun gun out of the man's hand before he could zap Brighton again.

"Stop playing around," a voice said. Brighton glanced up to see the butt of an M16 assault rifle just as it came down hard on his night-vision mask.

KRUNCH!!

Brighton saw stars and heard the sickening sound of shattered glass at once. Then he fell into total darkness . . .

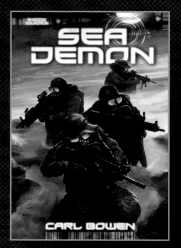

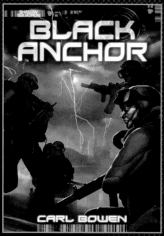

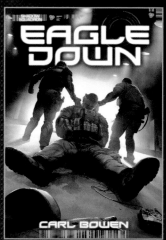

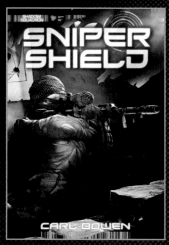

LOGGING OUT...

2012.101